Anderson Entertainment Ltd.\ GAP PLC © MMIV.
Original Production CAPTAIN SCARLET © 1967 ITC.
Captain Scarlet is used under licence by Granada Ventures Ltd

Published by Ladybird Books Ltd
A Penguin Company
Penguin Books Ltd, 80 Strand, London, WC2R ORL, England
Penguin Books Australia Ltd, Camberwell, Victoria, Australia
Penguin Group (NZ), cnr Airborne and Rosedale Roads, Albany,
Auckland 1310, New Zealand
All rights reserved

2 4 6 8 10 9 7 5 3

Ladybird and the device of a ladybird are trademarks
of Ladybird Books Ltd.

Manufactured in Italy

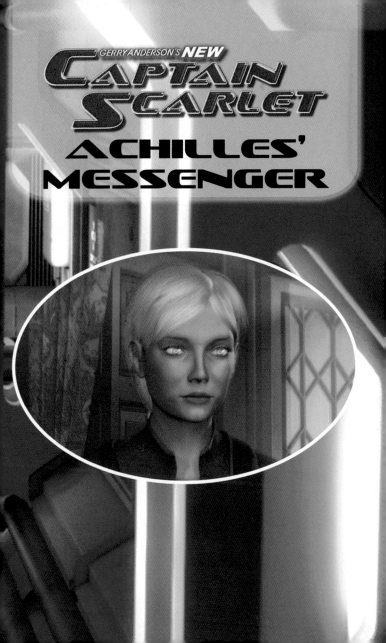

The interrogator aimed the spotlight into the prisoner's eyes. Again, he asked the question.

'The Skybase coordinates – what are they?'

Captain Scarlet, handcuffed and unshaven, squinted against the glare. His body was beaten, but his spirit remained unbroken.

'Captain Scarlet, Serial Number S700291160,' he spat out, defiantly.

'We're not even started with you yet, Scarlet,' said his tormentor, angrily. 'So make it easy on yourself – on everyone.'

A woman's scream came from nearby.
Destiny was being interrogated, too!
Scarlet's eyes flashed, but his resolve held.

His questioner had had enough – for now.
'Take him away!' he ordered, wearily.

As the guard behind Scarlet grabbed him
roughly, he fell. Lying on the floor of the
dingy cell, within his reach, was a nail. In
the instant before the guard dragged him
to his feet, Scarlet grabbed it.

The guard shoved Scarlet along a dimly lit passageway, flung him into a cell, and locked the door. Then he turned his attention to the other prisoner.

As the guard opened the door of her cell, the weak light fell on Destiny Angel. She, like Scarlet, was in bad shape.

'Waiting for a goodnight kiss, Princess?' said the guard, menacingly.

But a double-fisted blow from the hand-cuffed Captain Scarlet soon silenced him. Scarlet had used the nail to pick the lock of his cell, and come to rescue his friend. As he undid their cuffs with the unconscious guard's keys, Destiny mumbled bewilderedly.

'Paul ... but ...'

'Shhh – no time,' said Scarlet.

He quickly led her along darkened corridors, and out through a window into the moonlit grounds of the derelict Scottish mansion where they had been imprisoned.

Among the overgrown statues, a Trail Bike stood unattended. Destiny climbed on behind Scarlet. As he gunned the engines, an alarm howled into life.

'So much for a quiet exit,' said Scarlet.

Sure enough, as he swung the bike onto the narrow country road, two more bikes gave chase.

When speed didn't shake them off, Scarlet turned sharply onto a mud track, sending the lead pursuer skidding out of control.

The track led to a farmyard – and a dead end. Using a cart as a ramp, Scarlet jumped his bike across the farmhouse roof. The second rider attempted the same stunt – and crashed.

Back on the road, it seemed as if they were off the hook – until an oncoming Spectrum Rhino blocked their path. Its door opened and a uniformed woman emerged. She eyed Scarlet furiously.

'Captain Scarlet – what on earth do you think you're doing?'

Later, in the nearby Spectrum Training Base at Castle Balneath, Scarlet scowled as the woman – Astrid Winters – reprimanded him.

Winters ran the Interrogation Resistance exercise that he and Destiny had been on. She was livid with Scarlet for causing chaos by escaping from the training facility.

'Your people got sloppy,' said Scarlet, unrepentant. 'It's your people, Miss Winters, that need the training, not me.'

As he stormed out of her office, Winters' phone rang. Minutes later she was speeding away from the castle in her car, to an unexpected appointment.

But as she tried to slow down, her brakes failed. Her sports car plunged into the loch.

Twin green circles began to play on the water's surface. On the road, an exact replica of the sports car took shape, as if woven from thin air. A Mysteronised Winters was at the wheel.

By the time the replicated Winters had driven back to Castle Balneath, Captain Scarlet, exhausted, was flat out on the bed in his quarters.

Winters' eyes flashed Mysteron-green as she stealthily entered Scarlet's room, and crept towards him.

Scarlet was not easily surprised. Moments before Winters reached him, his eyes flicked open. Seeing her reflection in a mirror, he sprang into action.

But despite his combat expertise, he was no match for Winters. Showing inhuman strength and agility, she soon had him pinned down, her forearm across his throat.

Scarlet expected nothing but death. His eyes widened in surprise as Winters spoke.

'I'm not here to kill you, Scarlet. I've come to save you – you, and your planet.'

Minutes later, having sought out Destiny, Scarlet listened – warily – as Winters' replicant explained herself to them…

Back on Skybase Destiny explained the situation to Colonel White.

'She will only pass the details to you in person.'

The Colonel knew that any chance to find a Mysteron weakness must not be missed.

'If they do have an Achilles' heel, we can't dismiss the opportunity to discover it.'

And to gain their trust, Winters had offered a tip-off – the Mysterons, she claimed, were planning to blow up the World Science Congress.

At Castle Balneath, Scarlet kept watch over Winters as they awaited the Colonel's response. She was growing increasingly anxious, convinced that her fellow Mysterons would find out what she was up to, and come after her.

Her fears proved well-founded. A squadron of attack helicopters came buzzing out of the highland skies, spilling out Mysteron Stormtroopers into the castle grounds.

'If they catch me, you can't imagine what they'll do to me!' Winters told Scarlet, terrified.

'They'd better not catch you then,' he calmly replied.

They hurried through the castle corridors to a courtyard exit. Two Spectrum Rhinos were parked nearby. As they made a dash for one, Scarlet took a hit in the arm from a Stormtrooper's rifle. But some sharp shooting from Winters, who grabbed Scarlet's dropped pistol, saw them safely to the nearest Rhino.

Within moments of seizing the Rhino's controls, Scarlet had locked its missiles on the hovering Mysteron helicopters, and brought them crashing to the ground. He urged the Rhino forward, bursting through the castle's portcullis onto the open road.

But the second Rhino, with a Stormtrooper at its controls, gave chase. As Winters clung to her seat, Scarlet tore expertly along the winding road. Suddenly, he spun the vehicle through 180 degrees, and headed back at top speed towards the pursuing Rhino.

'Scarlet – what are you doing?' asked Winters, incredulous.

'Giving this guy the fright of his Mysteron life,' replied Scarlet.

The head-on collision tipped the enemy's vehicle on its side, and a nudge sent it tumbling into the loch beside the road. But the crash had disabled Scarlet's Rhino, too.

'Now what?' asked Winters.

'We walk,' said Scarlet, with a wry smile.

Meanwhile, at the World Science Congress building in New York, Captain Blue and Captain Ochre were following up Winters' tip-off.

'There's nothing here. We've been through the whole building, top to bottom to top again,' said Ochre, as she completed her scan for explosives on the skyscraper rooftop. 'If there was a bomb here, the locator would find it.'

Except, Blue suddenly realised, if the bomb was somehow shielded – and the rooftop water purification tanks would be an ideal place to conceal a device from electronic detection.

Sure enough, as they drained the first tank, a Mysteron bomb emerged, fixed to its floor.

Ochre's fingers flashed across her hand-held detector. 'According to my readings, it's going to blow in eight minutes.' she told Blue. 'We can't diffuse it in time!'

Moments later, Blue was at the controls of the Spectrum Hummingbird. He used its powerful winches to rip the water tank from its rooftop mountings.

Clamping the tank to the helicopter's belly, Blue set off at full tilt for the bay. He intended to make sure the Mysteron bomb exploded well out of harm's way.

'Four minutes, Adam,' warned Captain Ochre.

'Plenty of time to grab a take-out,' joked Blue.

But as they swooped between the buildings, another helicopter dropped in behind them, narrowly missing them with a missile. Mysterons!

Keeping his head, Blue managed to out-manoeuvre and shoot down their pursuer. But it cost time. As he released the tank over the bay, the bomb inside detonated.

The blast sent the Hummingbird plummeting out of control. Somehow, Blue pulled out of the dive. They'd done it!

Scarlet and Winters, meanwhile, were hiding out in a derelict mansion.

As they waited for help, Winters quizzed Scarlet about how he bore being half-human, half-Mysteron.

'I'm human,' insisted Scarlet. 'The Mysterons messed with me once, but that's just history.'

Winters looked unconvinced.

Suddenly, the sound of a Stormtrooper outside drew Scarlet's attention. But as he steadied his gun, the muzzle of another Stormtrooper's rifle pressed into his back.

Then, in an explosion of breaking glass, Destiny Angel burst through the window. She took out both Stormtroopers with well-aimed laser blasts.

Destiny looked at Scarlet and Winters and murmured, 'Looks like I got here just in time.'

On a rooftop, surrounded by bodyguards, Colonel White watched a Hummingbird touch down. Winters disembarked, flanked by Scarlet and Destiny.

'I'm sorry about the circumstances, but I'm sure you'll understand why we don't meet on Skybase,' said the Colonel.

'You still don't trust me' replied Winters. 'But you want to hear what I have to say.'

But before Winters could divulge her secret, a shot rang out. She slumped, clutching her chest.

Scarlet caught her in his arms. 'What is it Astrid – tell us,' he urged.

But Winters was consumed with terror. 'Don't let them get me Scarlet!' she screamed. Then, in a flash of green light, she vanished.

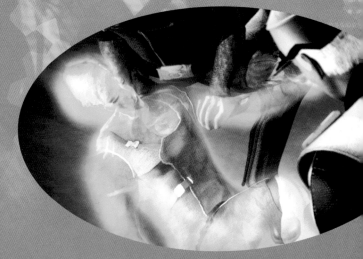

From a nearby vantage point, Captain Black trained his rifle sights on Scarlet, paused, then lowered his gun.

'No, Scarlet,' he mumbled malevolently. 'Not today. But one day. One day soon...'